HENRIETTA'S FIRST WINTER

Written and illustrated by
ROB LEWIS

THE BODLEY HEAD

LONDON

Henrietta was very young.
Her mother had died in the spring,
just after Henrietta was born.
She looked out at the autumn leaves.
She had never seen leaves turn yellow and brown before.

Other animals were busy collecting nuts and berries.
"Henrietta, you must store up food for the winter,"
they said. "In the winter the trees will be bare,
and there will be nothing to eat."

So Henrietta dug herself a store cupboard
and went out collecting nuts and berries to fill it.

The store cupboard was soon full.
Henrietta sat back in her chair and fell asleep.

She was woken by a splish, splash, splish, splash.
It was raining outside,
but the sound was coming from inside too.

She opened the store cupboard door.
With a whoosh, all Henrietta's winter food was
washed away, out of the front door,
and down the bank.

She mended the hole where the rain came in,
put on her boots,
and went out to collect more nuts and berries.

At last the cupboard was full again.
Henrietta made herself a hot drink,
sat by the fire and closed her sleepy eyes.

She woke up suddenly.
There was a munching sound coming from the cupboard.
Henrietta opened the door.

The cupboard was full of creepy, crawly creatures
eating her acorns, nuts and berries.
"Yum, Yum! Very nice!" they said.

She chased them outside.
Poor Henrietta.
All she had left was a pile of nutshells.
Tomorrow she would have to go out and collect some more.

The next day, the weather was cold and damp.
Nearly all the leaves had fallen from the trees,
and there weren't many nuts and berries left.
It would take Henrietta a long time
to collect enough to fill her store cupboard,
and she was very tired.

The other animals were watching Henrietta.
Out of their nests and holes they came.

They all helped to fill her store cupboard again.

Henrietta was so pleased that she had a tea party.
It was a great success.

But when everyone had gone home,
Henrietta found they had eaten all her food.

She looked out of her window.
Snow was falling. What could she do?
There were no more nuts and berries left.

She was very tired and very full of party food.
"I'll have just a little sleep,"
she said to herself.
"Then I'll see if I can find a few
scraps of food under the snow."
When she woke up . . .

It was spring!

For Tim – his first winter.

First Published in 1990 by The Bodley Head Children's Books
an imprint of the Random Century Group Ltd.
20 Vauxhall Bridge Road, London, SW1V 2SA

Random Century Australia Pty Ltd
89-91 Albion Street, Surry Hills, NSW 2010

Random Century New Zealand Limited
PO Box 40-086, Glenfield, Auckland 10, New Zealand

Century Hutchinson South Africa (Pty) Ltd
PO Box 337, Bergvlei, 2012 South Africa

Henrietta's first winter.
I. Title
823′.914[J]

ISBN 0-370-31410-7

Main text set in 20pt Baskerville by
Rowland Phototypesetting Ltd
Bury St Edmunds, Suffolk
Printed and bound in Great Britain
by Cambus Litho, East Kilbride